NOW I AM THREE!

by Jane Belk Moncure

illustrated by Linda Hohag

created by THE CHILD'S WORLD

 CHILDRENS PRESS, CHICAGO

Library of Congress Cataloging in Publication Data

Moncure, Jane Belk.

   Now I am three.
   Summary: A child demonstrates all the things a three-
year-old can do.
   [1. Growth—Fiction]   I. Hohag, Linda, ill.
II. Title.
PZ7.M739Nop   1984   [E]   83-20892
ISBN 0-516-01877-9 (Childrens Press)

NOW I AM THREE!

Now I am three.
Look at me.

I have three candles
on my birthday cake. . .
one, two, three!

I have three wheels
on my tricycle!
Watch me go.

I can pedal very
fast. . . or very,
very slow!

I can walk on a
walking board.

I can climb a tree.

I can ride on the
merry-go-round,
now that I am
three.

I can help
Mama shop. . .

and then put
things away.

I can zip my jacket. . .

and my boots on a
snowy, winter day.

I can paint pictures
with my brush.

I can make things
out of clay.

I can build lots of
things with blocks. . .

and help put the
blocks away.

I can wash some
clothes. I can hang
them out to dry!

I can hang onto my
kite and send it up
to fly.

Now that I'm three,
I can sing a song. . .

and I can play a drum
as I march along.

I like to play "dress-up."
How about you?

Do you like to play
"house" too?

Do you like to visit
animals in the zoo?

I like to pretend
that I'm one too!

There's more I can do now that I am three. . .

I can hold some baby animals very carefully.

And I can use
paper and glue. . .

to make surprises
just for you!

It's fun to be three!
There is so much
to do. Tell me, do
you like to be three
too?

31